Francis Waldron

**Free reflections on miscellaneous papers and legal**

**instruments under the hand and seal of William Shakspeare**

Francis Waldron

**Free reflections on miscellaneous papers and legal instruments under the hand and seal of William Shakspeare**

ISBN/EAN: 9783337278533

Printed in Europe, USA, Canada, Australia, Japan

Cover: Foto ©Andreas Hilbeck / pixelio.de

More available books at **www.hansebooks.com**

# FREE REFLECTIONS

### ON

# MISCELLANEOUS PAPERS

### AND

## LEGAL INSTRUMENTS,

#### Under the Hand and Seal of

## *WILLIAM SHAKSPEARE,*

#### IN THE POSSESSION OF

## *SAMUEL IRELAND,*

### OF NORFOLK-STREET.

---

" If circumſtances lead me, I will find
" Where truth is hid, though it were hid indeed
" Within the centre." HAMLET.

---

*To which are added,*
### EXTRACTS FROM AN UNPUBLISHED MS. PLAY,

#### CALLED

## THE VIRGIN QUEEN.

#### WRITTEN BY, OR IN IMITATION OF,

## *SHAKSPEARE.*

---

" Another yet ?——I'll ſee no more."
MACBETH.

---

### LONDON :

PRINTED FOR F. G. WALDRON,
At No. 18, Prince's Street, oppoſite Gerrard Street, St. Ann's.
M.DCC.XCVI.

# FREE REFLECTIONS,

## &c.

I N " *A Letter to George Steevens, Esq. by James Boaden, Esq.*" just published, is the following acknowledgement; which so exactly describes my own feelings in the same situation, that I take the liberty to adopt the very words.

" When a report first went abroad, that Mr. Ireland, of Norfolk-street, had made a discovery so important as the papers of Shakspeare, the writer of these sheets went to see them, and was very politely allowed by their possessor to hear him read them at leisure. In some instances credulity is no disgrace :—strong enthusiasm is always eager to believe. I confess, therefore, that, for some time after I had seen them, I continued to believe them genuine. They bore the character of the poet's writing—the paper appeared of sufficient age—the water-marks were earnestly displayed, and the matter diligently applauded.—

To

To a mind filled with the moſt ardent love and the moſt eager zeal, diſarmed of caution by the character too of the gentleman who diſplayed them, it will not be a ſubject of ſevere reproof, that the wiſhed impreſſion was made.

I remember that I beheld the papers with the tremor of the pureſt delight—touched the invaluable relics with reverential reſpect, and deemed even exiſtence dearer, as it gave me ſo refined a ſatisfaction. He, who has long combatted with the arts of literary impoſture, may ſmile at the ſimplicity of this avowal, although he ſhould be unable to refuſe his praiſe to the candour by which it has been dictated."

Such were preciſely *my* feelings when Mr. Ireland did me the favour to ſhew me the papers, &c. adverted to ; and I ſincerely hope, that nothing I may have occaſion to ſay concerning them, will be conſtrued into diſreſpect for him : their authenticity is now on trial at the bar of the publick, and every one is free to give evidence ; as mine will be faithfully delivered, I truſt it will be favourably received.

Unſkilled as I am, the only doubt that ſtruck me, on hearing the papers read, was of the word *whymſycalle* ; which, I then obſerved, I did not

remember

remember to have met with at fo early a period : this objection was foon overruled by the fuppofition that, as the word muft have been produced at fome period, Shakfpeare might then have coined it. I acquiefced, departed highly gratified, and in all other refpects ~~entirely fatisfied.~~ *convinced of their authenticity.*

In a converfation fome time after, on the fubject of thefe papers, with a gentleman†of the foundeft judgment, and beft information, I hinted the doubt I had entertained of the word *whymfycalle*; he pronounced it too modern for Shakfpeare : which, recollecting the adage *ex pede Herculem*, caufed me to look a little farther into the matter.

Moft of the obfervations I made, many of which, Mr. Boaden having anticipated me in them, are omitted, I am proud to fay, have been approved of by the gentleman alluded to. I fubmit the following, therefore, with a refpectful confidence, to the fkilful in Shakfpearean lore ; ftimulated by an irrefiftible impulfe to contribute my faint breath towards the difpelling thefe newly-arifen vapours : which, if fuffered to condenfe, might dim the effulgence of Shakfpeare!

In

In page 1, following the preface to, " *Miscel-laneous Papers,*" &c. is said, " for *I*, read *Aye* : *this was the Author's usual mode of writing.*"— Mr. Ireland might have added, *and of every other Author at that period.*

The superscription of queen Elizabeth's letter to Shakspeare, written with her own hand, is as carefully worded, as if it were to have been sent by the penny-post; had the office so named been then established. So far from directing a letter, Elizabeth wrote not the inward contents ; that haughty personage was not in the habit of such condescension : her signature only, or, on rare occasions, an additional line, comprised nearly the whole of her hand-writing, in any letter from her. In the letter the queen styles him " *Mas-terre* William ;" the orthography of that age was *Maister*, from the old French *Maistre*, now written *Maitre*; the French having ejected the *s* from many words in which we, though they are derived from them, retain it. This Chattertonism occurs frequently in these wonderful, or rather blunder-ful, papers.

" 50 *Poundes*" was a great sum, at that period, to receive for playing " *before the Lorde Leyces-terre* ;" although the " *Expenneces thereuponne*" amounted

amounted to " 19 *poundes*:" and, per contra, " 2 *fhyllynges moure*" to " *Mafterre Lowinne* ;" whom, in the " *Deed of Truft to John Hemynge*," Shakfpeare terms " *oure beft Actorr*;" was but a fmall compliment * " *forre bys Goode Servyces and welle playinge*." Even the fpelling of this cele- brated actor's name is dubious : in the lift of performers affixed to *Sejanus*, *The Foxe*, *The Alchemift*, and *Catiline*, (Ben Jonfon's Works, folio, 1616) his name is uniformly fpelt *Lowin* : and, furely, the perfon who entered into a legal contract with him, as Shakfpeare is, in thefe papers, reprefented to have done, muft have known the cuftomary orthography of his name.

It may alfo be obferved that the well-known urbanity of Shakfpeare's mind, and fuavity of his manners, could not have permitted him to affront the great Burbage, and other firft-rate performers, by unneceffarily ftyling Lowin, however excel- lent, in a legal inftrument of public notoriety, " oure *beft* Actorr."

---

* I remark here, en paffant, that *compliment*, in Shakfpeare's time, was ufed as a noun only ; in queen Elizabeth's letter to him it appears as a verb.

" Letter

"Letter to *Anna Hatherrewaye.*"

This female's names were *Anne Hathaway.* *Anna* is a Latin adoption of, comparatively, modern use; the orthography of *Hatherrewaye* is merely Chattertonian.

In the letter to her, a kingly crown is termed a "gyldedde *bawble.*" *Bawble* formerly meant the carved truncheon, with a fool's head at the top of it, ufed by court and ftage buffoons; therefore a very unlikely epithet to be applied by Shakfpeare to the fymbol of majefty; to which he every where pays great refpect.

In the "*Letter to the Earl of Southampton,*" we read "*itte is a Budde which Blloffommes Blloomes*" &c. Shakfpeare was too good a naturalift not to know, that a *Bud* firft *Blooms,* then *Bloffoms.*

"tooe *fublyme* a feeling," in the fame letter, is a very queftionable expreffion.

The fcrawl of this fublime and blooming letter is what fchool-boys call pot-hooks and hangers; and utterly unlike the hand-writing of that or any other age: and, if the fignature be the autograph of *any* earl of Southampton, it is, I am informed, not that of Shakfpeare's benefactor.

In

In the " *Profeffion of Faith*," " *acceeded toe*" is a phrafe an hundred years too modern for Shakfpeare.

Towards the conclufion of the " *Profeffion*" &c. *Chickenne* is ufed for the *Hen*, who receives her brood under her wings ; on the propriety of which confult the holy fcriptures. *Chickenne* is alfo objectionable in this place as ungrammatical, it being ufed in the fingular number ; whereas, the old fingular was *Chick*, and *Chicken* the plural. So *Ox*, and *Oxen* ; *Cow*, and *Cowen* ; contracted into. *Kine.*

In the " *Letter to Richard Cowley*" we read, " a *whymfycalle* conceyt ;"—the word *whymfycalle*, or *whimfical*, as I have already faid, does not, I am affured, occur in or near that period. I have a little book, printed in 1631, entituled " *Whimzies* : or a New Caft of Characters ;"* which, though

---

* The following extract from the character of " *A Ruffian*," in this fcarce book, as it relates to our ancient theatres, may not be unpleafing.

" To a play they wil hazard to go, though with never a rag of money : where after the *fecond Act*, when the *Doore* is weakly guarded, they will make *forcible entrie* ; a knock with a Cudgell is the worft ; whereat though they grumble, they reft pacified upon their admittance. Forthwith, by violent

affault

though *Whim* muſt apparently have preceded, is
the earlieſt inſtance I can recollect of any word
like *whymſycalle*.

One might imagine, from the careful ſuper-
ſcription of the letter to Cowley, that queen Elizabeth had condeſcended to direct that too.

The figure " *evidently meant for Shylock*" is
repreſented with a blue cap on.  Jews in Venice
are obliged to wear a red cap or hat, as a badge
of their perſuaſion.  Shakſpeare, however, or the
painter of this groteſque figure, might not be
acquainted with the coſtume of that place and
people.

In the " *Deed of Gift to Ireland*," after the
word " *followithe*" are three conjunctive notes of
admiration ! ! !  I believe two notes of admiration
in conjunction have not been uſed till very lately.
When the plays of " *Kyng henrye thyrde of Englande*," " *Kynge Hy* vii," &c. come to light, we
muſt

aſſault and aſſent, they aſpire to the two-pennie roome ; where
being furniſhed with Tinder, Match, and a portion of decayed
*Barmoodas*, they ſmoake it moſt terribly, applaud a prophane
jeaſt unmeaſurably, and in the end grow diſtaſtefully rude to
all the Companie.  At the Concluſion of all, they ſingle out
their *dainty Doxes*, to cloze up a fruitleſſe day with a ſinful
evening."

muſt not be ſurpriſed at finding in them the words ſwindler, ſhawl, and *Otabeite* ; or the * * * * of *Triſtram Shandy.*

As Shakſpeare's *Tempeſt* and *Macbeth*, which were given to Cowley, were never printed till the folio, 1623, was put forth by Heminge and Condell ; how chanced it that Heminge did not, having poſſeſſion of the " *Oakenn Cheſte*," with all the Plays therein, and being, we may imagine, on good terms with the party, prevail on " Maſterr Burbage," as he had done with Cowley, to per-mit him to publiſh " *yᵉ Virginn Quene*" in ſaid folio ?

For what reaſon did Heminge exclude from the folio Shakſpeare's " *newe Playe neverr yette impryuted called Kynge Hʸ VII*," which was " *toe bee whollye for ſᵈ J. Hemynge ?*" And why did not Heminge publiſh in that folio the " *Playe called Kynge Vorrtygerne*," and appropriate what the copy-right of it might then be deemed worth, to the uſe and advantage of " *thatt Chylde*" to whom it was aſſigned ?

The play of " *Kynge henrye thyrde of Englaude*" having, with " *Henry fowrthe*," " *Henrye fyfthe*," " *Kyng John*," and " *Kyng Leare*," been given by Shakſpeare to " *Maſterre William Henrye Ire-lande* ;

*lande* ; we may hope that Maſterre Samuel Ireland, or Maſterre Samuel-William-Henry Ireland, to whom we are obliged for the immaculate " *Kynge Leare*," will ſpeedily favour the publick with it: a play which Shakſpeare's " good and Worthye Freynd John Hemynge," to whoſe " honorr" he truſted, withheld, not only from a poor child, but from even himſelf, being already produced ; the other hitherto - unheard - of play, coming within the family-compact, " *ſame name and arms*," &c. is ſurely a leſs difficult attainment : and I conclude that the " *more intereſting hiſtorical Play*," announced in Mr. Ireland's preface, is the play of " *Kyng henrye thyrde of Englande.*"

Should any fortunate circumſtance reſtore to us " *Kynge Hy vii*," and who knows what induſtry and ingenuity may effect ? we ſhall probably poſ-ſeſs all the Dramas of Shakſpeare, hitherto mentioned ; as the writer of theſe Reflections, or what-ever they may be termed, is particularly acquainted with, and has great influence over, a now-living " *Maſterr Burbage*," lineally deſcended, we muſt ſuppoſe, from Shakſpeare's *Burbage*; through whoſe, or ſome other means, he doubts not he ſhall be enabled to recover an entire copy of " *ye Virginn Quene* :" from which he has already obtained a few extracts, ſubjoined to theſe remarks.

They

They are, for the reader's eafe, though not perhaps the antiquary's gratification, divefted of the ruft of age ; the redundant fpelling : but, let not a feeming lack of years be any impediment to a reverend eftimation.

The "*Tragedye of Kynge Leare,*" our Pfeudo-Shakfpeare fays, " *Ifse fromme Mafterre Hol-linnefhedde.*"

I have not a volume of that hiftorian at prefent in my poffeffion ; but, to the beft of my recollection, the orthography of his name in the title-page to his works is much more fimple.†

The " Libbertye" he has taken, Shakfpeare adds, in having " fomme lyttle deparretedde fromme hymme," " wille notte," he trufts " be blamedde bye" his " *gentle Readerres.*"

This is the firft inftance of Shakfpeare's appealing to *Readers* ; in writing his Dramas it is well known that he thought only of *Auditors* and *Spectators :* — but, as it neceffarily includes an implication that he had prepared this copy of " *Kynge Leare*" for the prefs himfelf, we might naturally expect the text to be correct ; at leaft intelligible ; fo far from which, it is, maugre Mr. Ireland's preface, the moft incorrect, unintel-

† *It is Holinshed.*

unintelligible téxt I ever faw, in any copy of any
play whatever: and, inftead of fuppofing, as fome
may, Mr. Ireland, his fon, or any other intelligent
perfon, the fabricator; I fhould rather imagine it
to be really, and bona fide, an ancient copy ; taken
furreptitioufly and erroneoufly, from the mouths
of the actors, by fome Printer's illiterate devil:
to which had, for private purpofes, been added
an imitation of Shakfpeare's fignature, and ad-
drefs to his " *gentle Readerres.*"

Mr. Ireland fays " that in the paper on which
this play [ " *Kynge Leare*"] is written, more
than twenty different water-marks appear."

If this be meant as evidence of the MS. of
" *Kynge Leare*" being the genuine production,
and hand-writing of Shakfpeare; I doubt it will
prove a weight in the oppofite fcale: when the
opulent Shakfpeare, as he undoubtedly was when
his *King Lear* was produced, fat down to write
a play, furely he was furnifhed with a quire or two
of paper for the purpofe; the fheets of which
would, of courfe, all bear the fame water-mark:
whereas, admitting the copy in queftion to be
an ancient, but ftolen, one; a needy hireling,
who could not afford better, may be fuppofed
to have written on cafually - collected and va-
rioufly - marked paper: and a modern fabricator,

cator; for argument' fake here imagined, would
be compelled to collect old paper piece-meal; in
all probability, containing " more than twenty
different water-marks."

In " *Kynge Leare*" p. 4. we read,
" Ande the whorefonne muſt be acknowleggede."
Shakeſpeare, if we may credit " *The Deed of
Truſt to John Heyminge*," could, like his own
Portia, better teach twenty what were good to be
done, than be one of the twenty to follow his own
teaching; otherwiſe he might have recollected
this paſſage in regard to " *thatte Chylde of whom
wee have ſpokenn butt who muſt not be named here*;"
and who, if ſuch " *Chylde*" ever exiſted, ſeems
to have been one whoſe ſervices ſtood bound to
*Goddeſſe Nature*.

The affectedly-antique ſpelling in " *Kynge
Leare*" is, throughout, ſo unprecedentedly redundant, as, of itſelf, to be a convincing proof
of inartificial imitation; but the ſpelling of the
Latin verb in the quotation, p. 4. " *Gloſterre
Exitte*," with the old Engliſh termination, the
double *t*, and *e* final, is ſo very ridiculous, that,
could it be proved to have been by Shakſpeare,
we might hereafter ſay, that he had ſmall Engliſh
and leſs Latin; as we have been taught by Ben
Jonſon to ſay, that he had ſmall Latin and leſs

C                    Greek

Greek: but, if he had any Latin, he muſt have ſpelt the word *Exit*, not *Exitte*. To have done, therefore, with " *Kynge Leare*," at leaſt for the preſent, the blunders, corruptions, omiſſions, interpolations, and ſophiſtications, warrant me in ſaying, that it is *impoſſible* for this MS. of " *Kynge Leare*" to have been the production and handwriting of Shakſpeare.

I fear I am not juſtifiable in commenting upon a ſuppoſed letter from Shakſpeare at Stratford, to a Printer or Bookſeller in London, read to me by Mr. Ireland, and not yet made publick,'relating to the play of " *Vortygerne*;" which informs us, that the price required for this perhaps-invaluable Drama was demurred at by the ſordid trader, altho' the Poet profeſſes to think it one of his beſt productions: but I hope I ſhall be pardoned, even by the poſſeſſor of the letter, for obſerving that " *The Deed of Truſt to John Hemynge*", in which '*Vorrtygerne*" is given to the unnamed " *Chylde*", is dated 1611; and, that the correſpondence between the Author and Trader is, I believe, ſtated or imagined to have occurred after Shakſpeare's retirement from the ſtage, to paſs the calm evening of his days at Stratford.

Strange !

Strange !—that the good, the grateful, the ge-
nerous Shakfpeare, fhould give a " *Playe neverr*
*yette Impryntedde,*" to a certain " *Chylde & hys*
*heires for everre*;" that he fhould then fet this
very play to fale for publication, at a period when
the value of plays depended on their not being
printed; and laftly, that, although the writings
of this unequalled genius were in his life-time
preferred before all others, and this was efteemed
by him his beft Play, his demand for it fhould not
have been " acceeded toe:" but, the immortal
Shakfpeare be reduced to the humiliation of re-
quefting that his favourite Play, and the correfpondence concerning it, fhould be tranfmitted
to him at Stratford upon Avon!

" *The Deed of Truft to John Hemynge*" and this
degrading correfpondence, furely, contradict each
other!—admitting the latter to be the fact, what
was Shakfpeare to do with his admired Play at
Stratford?—why not commiffion the perfon with
whom he had entrufted it, to deliver it to his friend
Heminge; that it might be acted in London, or
at Bank-fide, for the author or *Chylde's* emolu-
ment?—and not have his darling " *Vorrtygerne*"
thrown among lumber, in an obfcure country
retirement, to perifh through the ignorance of his
furvivors; or, be miraculoufly preferved, unfeen,
unheard-of, nearly two centuries: to enjoy, cum
multis

multis aliis, a kind of refurrection, in which the disjointed fragments of our Poet's mental part are fupernaturally gathered together, from " *mye Play offe Kynge Leare*" to a wager " *o 5 Shyllynges.*"

Having thus thrown out a few hafty reflections, I conclude with a fincere wifh; that, fhould *Vortigern*, or any other play imputed to Shakefpeare, poffefs merit enough to warrant the affumption; yet, by critical procefs be proved a forgery; the ingenious impoftor may be ranked with Chatterton in fame; but find better fortune than did that ill-fated, and ever-to-be-lamented youth !

EXTRACTS

# EXTRACTS

## FROM

# THE VIRGIN QUEEN.

IN the " *Deed of Truſt to John Hemynge*,"
publiſhed among the " *Miſcellaneous Papers*,"
by Mr. Ireland, is the following donation from
Shakſpeare.

" Toe Maſterr Burbage I give as followithe
from the Cheſte afs^d. mye two Playes of Cymbe-
lyne & Othello together withe mye choſen Interlude
neverr yette Impryntedd & wrottenn for & bye
deſyre of oure late gracyowſe & belovedd Quene
Elizabethe called ye Virginn Quene & playde 3
tymes before herreſelfe att the Revells ye profytts
from pryntyng ſame toe bee whollye for s^d. Burbage & hys hrs ſhoulde hee thynke fyttenne ſoe
toe doe."

It

It has been fuppofed, by fome who were inclin-
ed to think the " *Mifcellaneous Papers*" genuine,
that the Story of this chofen Interlude, as it is
termed, of *The Virginn Quene*, related to the hiftory of our Virgin Queen, Elizabeth, herfelf; but,
a woman of her mafculine mind could not have en-
dured to fee herfelf pageanted in a Stage-play, or
Interlude; and to have heard the fulfome adulation
with which a drama, reprefenting her own life and
actions, muft have been fraught: no; common
fenfe affures us, that the ftory muft have been
foreign to herfelf, and founded either on ancient
hiftory, romance, or fable; or, that it was invent-
ed by the poet.

The MS. from which the fubjoined extracts
are taken puts the matter out of doubt; *The
Virgin Queen* being an evident Sequel to *The
Tempeft;* and *Claribel*, a character therein, who
was married to the *King of Tunis*, being, for rea-
fons which are developed in the Drama, The *Virgin* Queen: that it was written by Shakfpeare I will
not take upon me to affert; yet, it is not likely that
any other perfon fhould attempt a Sequel to what
feemed fo perfectly concluded as doth the Tempeft: but, I may fafely fay, that if it were not written by Shakfpeare, it is written in direct imitation
of him.

Neither

Neither will I affert that it is the identical Interlude or Play mentioned in the " *Deed of Gift*;" for, I frankly acknowledge I had not thefe extracts from Mr. Ireland : they have been in their prefent owner's poffeffion twenty years; and the contents of the " *Mifcellaneous Papers*" may not have been in any body's poffeffion twenty months.

The play of *The Virgin Queen*, being, as hath been mentioned, a fequel to *The Tempeft*, refumes the ftory juft where it broke off ; and opens, on the morning fubfequent to the meeting and reconciliation of the Iflanders and the Neapolitan Voyagers, with an Invocation by Ariel of the Sprites, Fairies, Elves, Goblins, &c. in fubjection to Profpero, to affemble and bid adieu at his embarkation to their mafter. This fcene is chiefly lyrical.

After a Comick Scene between Trincalo, Stephano, &c. Profpero, Miranda, Ferdinand, and Caliban, enter.

Profpero, it feems, had intended to leave Caliban in comfortable poffeffion of his own cel! and moveables, in the Ifland ; but, that plan not according with the latter's feelings,. this dialogue enfues.

CALIBAN.

## CALIBAN.

No, 'pr'ythee, Profper, do not leave me here
'Mongft fiends and fpirits ; who, when thou'rt not by
To fhield him, will lone Caliban devour !

## PROSPERO.

Be fatisfied ;—there's nought to apprehend.
In Neptune's bed my magick volumes funk,
And many fathoms earth'd my broken ftaff,
Upon this ifle no fpirit will abide
Of good or evil, to delight or fear :——
Puppets and elves fhall gambol here no more,
In fportive ringlets, by pale Hecate's gleam ;—*
No more fhall hideous fpectres fcare thee home,
Loit'ring and grumbling at thy bidden tafk ;—
For, when I leave thee, thou'lt be more alone
Than when, with Ariel pent i' th' cloven pine,
A fhapelefs, helplefs thing, I prowling found thee.

## CALIBAN.

Which lonelinefs I now miflike and dread,
More than thy fprites and fiends ; I felt not, e'er
My noble lord came here, its irkfomenefs,
But thou haft taught it me : then leave me not,
I pr'ythee!—take me hence !—I'll lick thy feet,
And ever be obedient to controul.

* If this be the production of a modern, he ought to have known that *Hecate* is a tryffyllable ; Shakfpeare, indeed, ufes it as a dyffyllable only.

PROSPERO.

## PROSPERO.

What fays Miranda ? does my child approve
We take our late-offending vaffal hence ?

## CALIBAN.

Speak for me, Miftrefs! I'll be naught no more.

## MIRANDA.

I think, dear Sir ! the creature's much reform'd,
Since your forgivenefs of his laft offence ;
And, by commixture with fo many men,
He hourly humanizes ; pity 'twere
In lonefome wretchednefs to leave him now,
Perforce a favage to become again.

## CALIBAN.

Thanks! miftrefs! thanks!—thou fmooth-fac'd man,
fpeak too !

## FERDINAND.

'Pleafe you, Sir, take him hence ; I dare engage
He'll do you duteous fervice in return.

## CALIBAN.

Good now my king, be mov'd !

D                    PROSPERO.

## PROSPERO.

I am content ;
But, have a care! look you deferve this grace!

## CALIBAN.

Yea, that will I, in footh, my noble lord!
In the new world thou goeft to will I dig
For hidden fprings, to flake my mafter's thirft ;
Hew thee down fewel ; fcoop thee a trim cell ;
And be in all things meet thy vaffal true !

## PROSPERO.

Enough ;—endeavour to do well, good deeds
Will follow, and beget thee farther favour.

## CALIBAN.

Yet grant one other boon, and I am fped !
'Stead of this rugged hide, to 'ray me now
In fome fleek garment of my bounteous lord ;
Or ftill yon dolts thy flave will mooncalf call !

## PROSPERO.

'Twere not amifs ;—thou may'ft ;—but tarry not.

## CALIBAN.

I thank thy greatnefs !—I'll return anon,
And be thy lowly foot-licker for aye !

*Exit.*

Upon

Upon Caliban's return, dreſt in an old robe, Gonzalo, who in the interim had entered, and converſed with Proſpero, exclaims—

### GONZALO.

I'th'name of all that's ſavage, what comes here ?
The thing we ſpake of, ſurely, new-attir'd.
Why, how now, Sirrah ? Wherefore this fine change
From a rough ſkin to an embroider'd ſilk ?

### CALIBAN.

I crav'd this robe, that by yon ſcoffing apes
I might no more be flouted at, and mock'd ;—
They call'd me ſervant-monſter, mooncalf, fiſh !
Perchance they'll think I am more manlike now ;
It may be, but I am not near ſo warm:
A ſhaggy hide, from the chill breeze to 'fend,
Is far more worth than ſilk, or glitt'ring gold.

The entire company being aſſembled, and information brought that all is ready for their embarking, Proſpero ſays,

Here, then, I bid adieu to ſolitude !—
Farewell the deſert wild, the ſanded beach,
Where oft, from dawn to duſky e'en, I've ſtrain'd
My care-dimm'd opticks to deſcry a ſail ;
Farewell my low-roof'd cave, whoſe flinty bed
My humbled body hardineſs hath taught,
But never callous made my feeling mind ;
While ſome, whoſe limbs enervate upon down,
Permit their hearts to harden into ſtone.
Farewell adverſity ;—O, beſt of ſchools !

D 2

Still

Still may I practice what in thee I learn'd.
Farewell my forrows all!—hail, fmiling peace !
And laud we Heav'n for this our bleft releafe !

After a caution given to Profpero by Ariel, for
a very particular reafon affigned, not to touch at
any land till they had reach'd their place of defti-
nation, the whole company embark ; Spirits of
various denominations take leave of Profpero in a
Lyrical Farewell: which concludes the firft
Act.

In fome excellent papers on *The Tempeft*, in
*The Adventurer*, the writer of them, fpeaking of
the brutal barbarity of the fon of Sycorax, fays—
" I always lament that our author has not preferved
this fierce and implacable fpirit in Calyban, to the
end of the play ; inftead of which, he has, I think,
injudicioufly put into his mouth, words that im-
ply repentance and underftanding."

" —————I'll be wife hereafter
" And feek for grace." &c.

Whether the fine tafte of the elegant writer did
but coincide with Shakfpeare's then-unknown am-
plification of this fingular character ; or whether,
if it be an imitation only, the copier availed himfelf of Dr. Warton's hint, is a queftion for
the connoiffeurs : certain it is, that the implacable

cable fpirit of this demi-devil burfts forth, the firft opportunity it hath of again fhewing itfelf.

On Caliban's being affured, in the firft Act, that he fhall accompany his mafter, and ftill-beloved miftrefs, he fays, apart,

> Now fhall I fee the wond'rous, yearn'd-for, place,
> Where many Profpers and Mirandas dwell :
> He calls it Milan :—I opine 'tis Heav'n !
> It muft, perforce ; for many fuch as fhe
> Would make a Heav'n e'en of this defert ifle !

And when he firft fees the fhip, he exclaims,

> O, Setebos !
> What glorious thing is yon', as mountain huge !
> Doth firmly reft upon th'unftable fea ?
> Fanning, with flickering top, the welkin's cheek !
> 'Tis fure fome god, is come to bear us hence,
> To Milan ; which I rightly judg'd was Heav'n !

Being, in the fecond Act, on the deck, with Stephano and Trinculo, they converfe as follows ;—

### STEPHANO.

Now, 'Ban ! how do you ftomach failing ? is't not rare to fkim like a gull, thus, 'tween wind and water ? how doft like it, eh ?

### CALIBAN.

I like it much ! This is a brave, fine god !

And

And bears us daintily ;—how fwift he is !
' He feuds the ocean fleet as fawn the earth !
O, that my dam were living to behold him !
Grim Setebos fhe would renounce with fcorn ;
Low, proftrate, fall with me ; and thus adore !

                                [*Kneeling.*

### TRINCULO.

What's in the wind, now, 'trow ?

### CALIBAN.

Thou unmatch'd wonder !—miracle of pow'r !
Hear thy vow'd vaffal's pray'r, and grant his fuit !
Give me but vengeance on my tyrant lord,
(Whom, tho' I feign'd repentance; I deteft !)
And full fruition of his daughter's charms,
Thy bond-flave worfhipper I'll be for aye !

                                [*Rifing.*

### TRINCULO.

Lo ! the apoftate has got him a new idol, Stephano ; you
may return to your dog and bufh again ; he'll worfhip you
no more.

### CALIBAN.

What means this giddinefs ?—I cannot ftand !

### TRINCALO.

And mark, if the mooncalf be not drunk too !

### STEPHANO.

Out, you ninny !—'tis only the fhip's motion makes him
ftagger fo ; as it did me erewhile.

                                TRINCULO.

## TRINCALO.

By'r lady, and fo it may;—but a fherris-fack was mix'd with the fhip's motion when you caught the ftaggers.

## CALIBAN.

Sure I'm become what they call drunk again!
But know not how;—for, fave meer element,
Nought have I fwallow'd fince I left the ifle.

## TRINCALO.

See how he reels!

## CALIBAN.

I pr'ythee fhew where I may lie and fleep,
That Profper fee me not : elfe he will chide!

## STEPHANO.

Why, furely, the fhallow-brain'd ideot thinks himfelf drunk indeed!

## TRINCALO.

A rare conceit!—we'll humour it;—and, while he is napping, if we can find the old necromancer in the mood, try to get off keeping watch here at night.

## STEPHANO.

Agreed.—Come along, you drunken owl! and we'll lead you where you may rooft in fafety, till you are fober.

## CALIBAN.

But am I drunk in footh ?—I pr'ythee fay!

TRINCALO.

### TRINCALO.

Drunk, quotha ? there's *the* queftion !—ay, reeling-ripe,
as when the piping fairy led us by the ears into the pool ;
then, indeed, it was with fack : now with only the fhip's
motion :—but, a fmall matter will turn a weak head !

### CALIBAN.

Give me fack now ! for I can but be drunk !
'Twill drown my fear, and make me full of mirth ;
I may as well be jocund-drunk, as fad :—
Give me fome fack, I pr'ythee, ere I fleep !

### STEPHANO.

Here's a flaggon for you, fifh !—the king in the cabin
can't drink ~~drink~~ better.

### CALIBAN.

'Tis paffing good ! a king 'twill make of me !
*my* This fhall be pillow be ;—I'll drink and fleep ;
Nor dread four Profper, while of this I've ftore.

—

Trincalo and Stephano having in their appli-
cation to Profpero told him that Caliban was
drunk and afleep, are orderd to fetch him ; they
aroufe, and bring him into the cabin.

### CALIBAN.

Whither doft lead me ?—what, doth Profper fleep ?
And fhall we brain the hated tyrant now !

### PROSPERO.

Approach, thou earth ! thou drunken, murd'rous flave !

### CALIBAN.

CALIBAN.

Thou ly'ft ! I am no flave;—but free as thou!
If I perchance am drunk; 'twas this huge god;
Whofe man-fed belly we are now within,
Did make me fo while I did worfhip him.
Muft I be ever thus for nothing chid!

Profpero, to punifh his relapfe, enjoins him to
remain on the deck, with the others who had
offended him, all night.

They endeavour to footh, and reconcile Caliban
to what they have brought on him, by fome com-
mon-place jefts; but the monfter, not being now
in a joking humour, fays—

Peace, ye dull fools! I will no more endure
This fcurvy jefting;—ye are bafe and falfe!
Ye firft, like fiends, feduce, and then betray !
Beware, foul traitors, how henceforth ye mock;
Left into both I ftrike my fharpen'd fangs,
And 'gainft each other dafh ye, mongrels, dead !

They pacify him at length, by promifing to
devife fome revenge againft Profpero; and he
exclaims,—

The thought of that would make me brave the night,
Tho' livid light'nings, darting, finged my head;
And rifted rocks 'mid yefty waves o'erdafh'd!

He is, at length, wrought into good humour;
and the fecond act concludes with their finging

E                                        the

the entire catch, of which in *The Tempeſt* we have only this fragment ;————

"Flout 'em, and ſkout 'em ; and ſkout 'em, and flout 'em ;
"Thought is free."

The "*gentle Readerres*" muſt ſuppoſe other ſcenes to have intervened ; but Caliban being ſo unique a character, I was ſolicitous that the extracts I procured ſhould relate chiefly to him : in the third Act he is ſeen dreaming of Miranda, and talking in his ſleep, on the deck ;————

Ho, ho! 'tis heaven !—now I am bleſt indeed !

————————

Kiſs me again, my ſtar-eyed Paragon !
Thy mouth's more ſweet than luſcious honey-bags.

————————

Come with me, ſwan-ſkin ! and I'll ſhew thee where
Theſe nails have dug for Proſper a deep pit,
Falſe-ſurfac'd quaintly with inviting herbs ;
Within lurk adders, urchins, ſcorpions, toads !
That, if i' th' fall the tyrant be not kill'd,
By venom'd bites and ſtings he'll mad expire !

The Spirit of his Dam, Sycorax, deſcends, amidſt thunder, lightning, &c.

Caliban

Caliban awakes.

O, Setebos, what a rare dream was this!
To kifs my miftrefs' honey-dropping lips,
And—Day and Night!—do I yet fleep or wake?
Wing'd like a bat methinks I fee my dam!
In dreams I have oft beheld thee, but ne'er thus;
Thou wilt not harm me, Sycorax?—lo, I kneel!

Sycorax, who at her death was " *doom'd for a certain term to faft in fires*," replies——

Fear not, my fon! this very hour
Was Sycorax freed; a Spirit of pow'r!
On earth to rule almoft divine!
This watry element's not mine.
Then, if thou hat'ft thy tyrant lord,
Unto thy mother's heft accord.
To drive him fwift into my toil,
By force, or by fome fubtle guile,
The pilot caufe fteer ftraig for land;
There nothing can my power withftand!
A forcerefs, at my bidding, there
E'en now his torments doth prepare:
And, to protect thee from annoy,
Invulnerable be, my joy!

Sebaftian and Anthonio, having returned to their villainy, abet the monfter; whofe firft ftep to diftrefs Profpero is the deftroying, or throwing over-board, all the provifions; excepting what is neceffary for himfelf and his party.

Profpero

Profpero and the reft, being informed of thefe
difafters, repair to the deck; Caliban thus ex
ults over his mafter :———

> Ho, ho, ho, ho ! I now fhall be reveng'd
> For all my pinches, ftitches, racking cramps !
> My unthank'd fervices, and toilfome tafks !
> Bearing huge logs of wood, for needful fire
> To drefs the meat I firft had hunted down ;
> From the quick frefhes fetching wholfome drink ;
> For lufcious fhell-fifh, or choice callow birds,
> Climbing fteep craggy cliffs, and brittle boughs ;
> From which when I have fall'n, and gotten hurt,
> To heal my wounds thou, tyrant, gave'ft me blows !

During the altercation, Ferdinand fays ;—

> ——————————let us, my friends,
> Affail the triple knot ; and, when fubdu'd,
> Teach them the way to faft, as they would us.

### CALIBAN.

> Try firft to mafter me, weak, ftripling boy !
> I guard the food, eke moft delicious wine ;
> O'ercover'd with this now-defpifed robe !
> And, 'lefs on land ye go in fearch of more,
> Ye, famifhing, fhall fee us glut and gorge,
> Whilft, ravenous grown, each other ye devour !

### PROSPERO.

> Foul hag-feed, hence ! down to the hold, begone !

### CALIBAN.

> Begone thyfelf, proud tyrant ! I'll not budge.
> My cruel mafter thou haft been too long !

I now

I now am thine!—and, if thou difobey'ft,
The ftripes and pinches thou inflict'd'ft on me,
On thy curft flcfh will I, tenfold, repay!

## PROSPERO.

How now, bold flave! this language to thy lord?
Who, with a word, can ftrike thee, inftant', dead!

## CALIBAN.

Thou ly'ft! thou canft not—vain, forgetful fool!
Thy fpells, thy charms, yea all thy pow'r is gone;
Which did controul the great and leffer light,
Subjected Spirits, and made me thy flave!
In that fame fea thy potent magick ftorm'd,
Like a dull thing thou drowned'ft all thine art!
Now Caliban, more ftrong, is Profper's lord;
And thou muft him obey, as he did thee.

The good old lord, Gonzalo, during the conteft fays,——

Of forty devils were the pow'r combin'd,
Thus would I ftrive to quell this hell-born beaft!

## CALIBAN.*

Ho, ho, ho, ho! thy fword is blunt, old man!
Now could I grind thy pithlefs bones to duft;
Rend ye to fhreds, or tread ye into earth!

But,

---

* Could any thing really perfuade me that an original and hitherto-
unpublifhed play, written by Shakfpeare, were in being, two paffages in
this fpeech would; which are fo fimilar to two others in *Macbeth* and
*As you like it*, that it is not probable any imitator would have ventured on
fuch clofe parallels.

But, get ye gone !—ye may as foon wound air,
Water, or fire, as charmed Caliban !
The fpirit of my dam is ftrong in me!
Hath callous made me to weak mortals' blows ;
And your united force I ftand, and dare!
Ho, ho, ho, ho ! what, are ye all afeard ?

### GONZALO.

By'r Lakin ! I yet never was before ;
But my old blood's now curdled in my veins :

### PROSPERO.

Put up your fwords, good firs, they're but as ftraws ;
A charmed life, in aid of ftrength, now given,
This beaft hath pow'r to bring us all to nought !
My life alone fell Sycorax doth feek ; —
And that, to fave you, will I gladly yield !
Thou more-than-devil ! fpeak thy dam's beheft ;
Which, though deftruction follow, I obey !

### CALIBAN.

Make ftraight to land, dread Sycorax commands !
What there fhall hap I know not ;—but, I have hope
All but thy daughter will my dam deftroy !
My fruftrate-purpofe then will I effect,
And people th' unknown clime with Calibans !

### FERDINAND.

Peace, monfter, peace ! that heav'n will ne'er permit.

### PROSPERO.

Patience, my fon ! my life alone is fought ;
And what's a life, compared with chaftity,
Connubial crown ! we come and go as faft,

*As

\*As mill-fail fhadows courfe each other o'er
The funny earth, in an unceafing round!
Nor can I perifh, but by that decree,
To which who would not chearfully refign !
For land, ho ! pilot ; fearlefs I'll afhore,
To prove the utmoft malice of the fiend!
Lament not, fhould I fall ;—they are not ills,
Tho' they appear fuch, righteous heaven wills !

The Scene clofes, and the third act concludes with a convocation of Ariel, and other good Spirits; who having determined to counteract, if poffible, the machinations of Sycorax, &c. fing a hymn and chorus, expreffive of their ardour in the caufe of Virtue.

The fourth act brings us acquainted with Abdallah, (in *The Tempeft* the namelefs) King of Tunis, lately married to Claribel, daughter of Alonfo, king of Naples.

In an old geographical book in my poffeffion, date unknown, is the following paffage ;—

"This

---

\* As mill-fail fhadows &c.

This paffage ftruck me, at firft, as too mean and familiar for the mouth of Profpero; till I recollected an almoft-fimilar one in the firft act of *The Tempeft* ;

"‌—————————where thou didft vent thy groans,
" As faft as mill-wheels ftrike."

" This whole Countrie (at this day) is called the kjngdom of *Tunis:* the king whereof is a kinde of ftipendary unto the *Turke:* the people that inhabite there are generally *Sarázens,* and doe profeſſe *Mahomet.*"

It has always appeared very ftrange to me, yet I have never met with any obſervation on it, that Shakſpeare ſhould ſo groſsly have erred againſt the known laws and cuftoms of nations, as to couple the daughter of a Chriftian king with a Mahometan!

For a royal Proteftant to marry a Papift, or vice verſa, required a diſpenſation from the Pope; but, to permit the union of a Chriftian princeſs and an infidel was, I believe, only in the power of a Poet; who ~~could~~ might plead in extenuation, that " *the trueſt poetry is the moſt feigning.*" We ſhall find, however, by this *Sequel,* that Shakſpeare, if it be his, was not inſenſible of the faux pas he had committed; as the marriage is ſo very infelicitous, that the Bride, poor thing! remains a *Virgin:* whence the title of this choſen Play or Interlude, THE VIRGIN QUEEN.

" 'Fore the beginning of this play," a Sorcereſs, (formerly leagued with Sycorax, who was baniſhed from Argier, or Algiers, to Proſpero's iſle)

isle) was enamoured of Abdallah ; he rejecting her
offers of love, and marrying Claribel, the enraged
witch prevents confummation ; conveys the unhappy pair by her *" fo potent art"* from Tunis,
and holds them in durance : but, for that even
Magick cannot quite feparate a loving married
pair, they are permitted to fee and converfe with
each other daily.

In this pofture of affairs the fourth Act opens ;
difcovering Abdallah alone, reclining in a fump-
tuous pavilion.

### ABDALLAH.

Nights vapours are difpers'd ; and the clear morn
Blufhes like bafhful bride from couch upris'n ;
Whofe yellow treffes, all difhevell'd, throw
A golden glare around, creating day !
But what is day after drear nights like mine ?
From my fweet bride eftrang'd, my Claribel !
Yet, wherefore do I thus indulge defpair ?
Still may I hope to be deliver'd hence ;
Still hope I fhall regain my throne and crown ;
From which, as in a dream, my queen and felf
By Hyrca's forcery were hither brought,
Me for her paramour ; detefted hag !
And my fair bride her low-degraded flave !
But, foft ! I hear the hafteful ftep of love !
'Tis Claribel ! fly forrow from my breaft !
For where fhe comes nought can abide but joy !

*Enter Claribel.*

F                    CLARIBEL.

## CLARIBEL.

My dear Abdallah ! mine and Tunis' lord !
Fain would I greet thee with a happy day ;
But the fell Sorcerefs, Hyrca, wild with ire,
That her foul paffion ftill you treat with fcorn,
Since midnight hath been working fpells, and charms,
The prelude of refolv'd deftruction nigh !

## ABDALLAH.

Were't but myfelf her wicked pow'r could reach,
I'd meet her utmoft fury with a fmile ;
Yielding my firm and unpolluted flefh
By fiery pincers to be burnt and torn !

## CLARIBEL.

And thinks my love that only him would harm ?
Thou know'ft whate'er of ill fhould thee betide,
Muft wound the foul of doating Claribel !
But, for fome hope to mitigate this fear,
As on the ocean's marge e'en now I gazed,
I faw a gallant veffel furl her fails ;
Whilft from her boat ftept divers on the fhore :
And fee, dear lord, already they approach.

*Enter Profpero and Miranda.*

## MIRANDA.

'Befeech you, Sir ! venture no farther on !

## PROSPERO.

Fear nothing, dear !—lo, yonder are a pair,
Of human form, and moft majeftic port ;
I will accoft them.

MIRANDA.

## MIRANDA.

Rather, Sir, avoid them !
They're fpirits ! and, tho' one feems fair and good,
That, with fo dark an hue, is fure a fiend !

## PROSPERO.

Collect thyfelf, my child !—'tis but the tinct
Peculiar to the race in Africk born,
Upon which coaft we now in fafety tread ;
E'en fuch a one, yet courteous as ourfelves,
Did Ferd'nand's fifter, Claribel, late wed :
Should this man prove like what Fame blazons him,
And from fell Sycorax' malice Heav'n doth fhield,
We cannot doubt of fuccour in our need.

## CLARIBEL.

Heard you, Abdallah, what this ftranger faid ?

## ABDALLAH.

I did ; and am abforb'd in wonder, fweet !
'Pleafe you, approach, grave Sir ! and you, fair maid !
Nor lack for aught, fave what we alfo want.

*Enter Ferdinand, his fword drawn ; and, foon after, Alonzo, Gonzalo, Adrian, and Francifco.*

## FERDINAND.

The beaft no longer feems invulnerable,
But fhuns my fword ; and, with his foul compeers,
Growling, a different track from us purfues.

PROSPERO.

## PROSPERO.

To fhare my fortunes fince ye all perfift,
As yet, 'thank Heav'n ! we are not only fafe,
But landed on a feeming plenteous fpot ;
Where are inhabitants, of manners mild
As their foft climate's fweet furrounding air.

## ALONSO.

The Moorifh king, Abdallah, and my child !-
'Tis fure enchanted ground !—Are we in Tunis,
A delufive dream,—or, is it witchcraft all ?

## GONZALO.

Witchcraft, I doubt ! and thefe but devils, Sir,
Hid in your children's fhapes.

## ALONSO.

Art thou my child,
An infubftantial fhade, or wicked fiend ?

## FERDINAND, *embracing Claribel.*

Shade is it none, but Claribel herfelf ;—
No fiend had ever pow'r to look fo fair !

## CLARIBEL, *kneeling to Alonfo.*

Aftonifhment hath held me dumb till now !—
'Tis your own Claribel, your wretched child !

## ALONSO.

Ha ! wherefore wretched ? Speak, ungrateful king !
Did I deprive our Europe of thofe charms,
To have my child in Tunis wretched made ?

CLARIBEL.

## CLARIBEL.

Oh, no! alack, Sir, we are far from thence !

## ABDALLAH.

Great king of Naples ! my moſt honour'd ſire !
Whom to behold again, was paſt my hope ;——
Fly with your goodly company this place,
And reſcue hence your Claribel and ſon !
But, if that may not be, ſecure yourſelves.

## ALONSO.

What means my ſon ! know you of ill awaits ?

## ABDALLAH.

Here 'bides a potent Sorcereſs ; by whoſe art
From Tunis we were hither ſtrangely brought,
Soon as your royal fleet had homeward ſail'd ;
Myſelf the object of her foul deſire,
My virgin-bride degraded to a ſlave !
Her the vile witch would elſewhere fain have ſtay'd,
But had not pow'r ; and, though till now debarr'd
Chaſte Hymen's rites, on each returning morn
Like th'eaſtern ſun ſhe glads my longing eye !
For witchcraft cannot quite divide the pair,
Whoſe hearts by love and wedlock are entwin'd !

## PROSPERO.

Myſterious Heav'n ſure pointed out this path
To free from hence theſe twain ! my mind's at reſt !
Let us, my friends, ſtraig victual home our ſhip ;
And, nought impeding, quickly re-embark.——
Come, I'll inſtruct you, Sirs, how to enſnare

The

The fkipping kid, and dappled, bounding fawn ;
Whilft younger Ferdinand doth agile climb
The cliffs and trees, for birdlings nefted there.

### FERDINAND.

Miranda, fweet ! ftay thou with Claribel,
Thy Ferdinand's lov'd fifter, and now thine ;
I muft accompany our fires and friends,
Swift as the roe-buck to outftrip our game !

### ABDALLAH.

I'll guide you, Sirs, to where you'll plenteous find
The finn'd or feather'd race ; unto the haunts
Of the fleet venifon, the clamb'ring kid,
And, though to flaughter them doth irk my heart !
The lambkin, frifking near his fleecy dam :
Or, if a nobler game you would purfue,
The boar, fierce buffalo, and angry bear.*

### PROSPERO.

Lead on, great Sir ! 'twill be a royal chafe,
Wherein a king doth roufe for us our game !
Stay with this fair one, chuck ! nor fear mifchance.
This wond'rous meeting Heav'n, I'm fure, defign'd
The foretafte of ftill greater blifs in ftore !

                    [*Exeunt all but Claribel and Miranda.*

### CLARIBEL.

Stranger ! with whom my Ferdinand feems charm'd,
Say, whence and who thou art ?—a queen ?—his bride ?
Whom, fince my nuptials, he hath woo'd and wed ?

                              MIRANDA.

---

* I fear that Shakfpeare, or his imitator, has, in this enumeration of
creatures, mentioned fome not indigenous to the northern coaft of Africa ;
where the fcene is now fuppofed to lie.

## MIRANDA.

Anfwer me firft.—Why did you kifs my love ?
I much admir'd, till then, your angel-face !
Are you an angel, or of woman-kind ?
For nought to judge by faw I e'er before ;
Except the mocking fhadow of myfelf,
And Ariel, my grave fire's angelick fprite ;
You moft refemble me, tho' fairer far !

## CLARIBEL.

Thy fpeech is paffing ftrange ! but, if't be footh,
Thy innocence deceives thee overmuch.
No more can I, a woman as thou art,
Compare with thee, fairer than beauty's queen,
Than can with Ferdinand the Moor, my lord ;
Whom, ne'erthelefs, paft health or life I love !

## MIRANDA.

What, that dark creature !—'tis not poffible ;—
As foon the fwan may on the raven dote !

## CLARIBEL.

I thought like thee when firft the Moor I faw,
And almoft loath'd where duty bade me love ;
But my Abdallah has a fnow-white foul,
Which o'er his hue a bleaching luftre throws ! *
'Thas won that heart Alonfo could not give,
And chang'd my meer obedience into choice.
Then be not jealous, faireft ! thou'ft no caufe ;
Much as a fifter fhould I Ferd'nand love,
But truly, no jot more.

* This reminds us of Defdemona's expreffion :—
    " I faw Othello's vifage in his mind."

MIRANDA.

### MIRANDA.

Jealous! what's that ?
Is it a Naples, or a Tunis word ?
I know not what it means ;—but am content !
So kind you look, and fair you fpeak, I'm fure
You cannot mean to do me any wrong.

### CLARIBEL.

Come, then, fweet-heart ! and, in the adjacent bow'r,
Repofe thee 'till our lords and fires return ;
Tafte of the pine, or more nutritious fig ;
Whilft the pomegranate and fharp citron's juice,
Temp'ring each other, form thy mingled draught.

### MIRANDA.

Shew me, I pray, to the clear, running ftream ;
With, if you have't, a little new-drawn milk ;
Some berries, cracknels, or ripe ears of corn ;
And, our Creator thanking firft, then thee
For thy much goodnefs to a ftranger-maid ;
I'll break my faft, nor covet daintier fare !

Caliban, with the two villains, Anthonio and
Sebaftian, having remained perdue, enter, and
fuddenly feize the unguarded females ; a conteft
enfues between the three brutes on their account :
Anthonio claiming to have Claribel, and Sebaftian attaching himfelf to Miranda.

### CALIBAN.

But whom fhall I have, if you each take one ?
My miftrefs have I ever hunger'd for !

Sty'd

Sty'd in a rock with her, on acorns fed,
Sea-brine, or ftagnant, mantled-pool, to drink,
On her alone I, gluttoning; could have gorg'd,
And nothing lack'd, having my nonpareil!

[*Attempting to clafp Miranda.*

### MIRANDA.

Save me, Anthonio! fave your helplefs niece!

### ANTHONIO.

My charge is here;—Sebaftian you will fhield.

### SEBASTIAN.

Forego your hold!—Miranda muft be mine!
The other female, if Anthonio lift,
Thou'rt free to take; but this I'll guard with life!

### CALIBAN.

'Tis well there is another to appeafe,
Elfe her I'd have, or will or nill ye, lord!
This is as red and white, and finer far!
Wilt thou be mine, my jay, my parroquet?
Thou'rt wond'rous gaudy; I fhall love thee much!*

### ANTHONIO.

Stand off, fir brute! this is my lovely prize;—
Miranda you declar'd was your defire;—
Her muft you have, or none!

* This filthy monfter having, in *The Tempeft*, fuggefted to Stephano
that he might poffefs Miranda; it is not to be wondered at, that he is
here content to exchange her for Claribel.

## CALIBAN.

Oh, oh, oh, oh !          [*Roaring tremendously with anger.*

## CLARIBEL.

Heav'n, what a conteſt !

## MIRANDA.

No way to eſcape ?

## CALIBAN.

What, am I both denied ?—then, both I'll have !
Your holds forego, and quit them ſtraiɡht to me,
Or, by my dam's god, Setebos, I ſwear,
I'll flay ye, quick ! then tear you joint from joint !*

*(Caliban ſeizing the men, the females get free.)*

## CLARIBEL.

Fly, fly !   Abdallah !

## MIRANDA.

Ferd'nand ! father ! friends !

[*Exeunt, ſeverally.*

## CALIBAN.

Let looſe, ye barnacles ! they both are flown !

* I'll flay ye quick ! &c.—*Quick* may here ſignify either *alive* or *imme-
diately*; the former I conceive to have been the Author's idea, as it gives
the more ſpirited and ſavage meaning. *I'll flay you alive*, is a common
expreſſion from vulgar parents and nurſes to froward children.

ANTHONIO.

### ANTHONIO.

We hold thee not !—'tis thou detaineſt us !
Darting your talons through our robes and ſkins,
Which you can ſcarce withdraw !

### SEBASTIAN.

I'm ſtruck to th'bone !

### CALIBAN.

Thus, then, I wrench them forth !

### ANTHONIO and SEBASTIAN.

Oh !————

### CALIBAN.

Howl ye ?  dogs !
If I could tarry I would give ye caufe ;
And into atoms rend your quivering hearts !

*[Exeunt, feverally.*

Comick matter now, as throughout the play,
takes place ; which relieves the weight and terror
of the ferious fcenes.

The fifth Act commences with the Monſter,
in purſuit of the females.

### CALIBAN.

I can find neither ! and could tear myſelf
For letting them, fo dolt-like, both efcape !
Had I kept either of them 't had fuffic'd ;

G 2

Though

Though my own miftrefs leifer I'd enjoy !*
Nor can I fpy my dam! I hop'd t'have feen
'The wond'rous fpirit, when we reach'd the land,
Deftroy that tyrant Profper! or, while-ere,
I had done?t upon the fea! but, what comes here ?
Methinks I hear a footfall in yon dell ;
Perchance it is my miftrefs ;—that it may !
I will enbufh me ! then, fhould fhe approach,
Like cat-a-mountain fpringing, feize my prey !

### MIRANDA, *entering.*

Whither, ah whither fhall I bend my fteps,
To feek my ftraying father and dear lord ?
Or hide me from—Proteft me, heav'n ! I'm caught !

### CALIBAN.

'Scape if thou can'ft again ! now thou art mine,
'Spite of thofe chattering and deceitful apes ;
Who would have talk'd me out of thee, my right !
Or that much finer, but lefs beauteous, fhe.

### MIRANDA.

Be gentle, Caliban !—gripe not fo hard !
Left with your talons my frail fkin you tear !

### CALIBAN.

I cannot harm thee !—tho' I meant thee fcathe,
In punifhment for thy late fcornful flouts!
Be thou but kind, I will be fo to thee !

### MIRANDA.

* This erotick ufe of the verb *enjoy*, I thought not Shakfpearean, till I
recollected the following paffage in *King Lear :*——
    " ————neither can be enjoy'd,
    " If both remain alive."
Yet, can it be imagined that Caliban could have learnt it, with this peculiar and indelicate fenfe, from his only teachers, Profpero and Miranda ?
I fear the author, whether ancient or modern, in this inftance forgot
himfelf.

## MIRANDA.

Alack, alack ! when was I otherwife ?

## CALIBAN.

Full oft to me ! although I ever lov'd,
And fondled thee !—When firſt into my iſle
Proſper, a puling babe, Miranda brought ;
Weeping through hunger, ſhiv'ring with bleak winds ;
I lick'd the tears from thy frore, blubber'd cheeks,
Noufled and chafed thee in my hairy arms,
Hugging thee clofe as marmofets their young ;
Fed thee with eggs ;—into thy pretty mouth
From the goat's dug prefs'd the warm, foſt'ring milk ;
Of thiſtle-down and gofs'mer made thy bed ;
Then huſh'd and lullaby'd thee to thy ſleep,
And lack'd my own, that thine might be fecure.

## MIRANDA.

I ever ſtrove to thank thee for't ; and ſtill,
As from my father fpeech and fenfe I learn'd,
Delighted in imparting both to thee !
I never laid upon thee harſh command ;
Affiſted always to trim up our cell ;
And, in each look, word, deed, was ever kind !

## CALIBAN.

But kinder far to Ferdinand ! though he
Ne'er nurs'd, nor ſtroak'd, nor fed, nor fondled thee !
In our lime-grove I lurk'd behind a buſh,
And faw the lack-beard kifs that down-like hand ;
I could have claw'd his lips off, had I dar'd !
But now, from Proſper's magick-pow'r I'm free ;
Him and my hated rival laugh to fcorn ;
Here have thee, and will make thee ſtrait my own !

MIRANDA.

### MIRANDA.

O, Ferdinand! my love! where haſt thou ſtray'd?
Haſte, and deliver me from this vile thrall!

### CALIBAN.

'Twere death, ſhould Ferd'nand interrupt me now!
Though I ſeem'd fearful late, and ſhunn'd his ſword,
'Twas but in craft, to compaſs what hath happ'd;
Then ſtint this din, aud let thine eyes ſoft beam;
Nor ſcorn,' nor flout, for I'm not ſmooth as he!
In beauty what I lack I have in ſtrength;
More needful, to protect and get thee food!
I'll fetch thee, miſtreſs! ſweet birds from the grove;
Gather th'empurpled grape for thy repaſt;
And weave a flow'ry garland, thee to crown
Queen of this unknown clime and me, for aye!
Give me the honey of thy lips in lieu,
And let me clip thee!

### MIRANDA.

Monſter! ſtand aloof!
I feel ſtrange courage, and unuſual ſtrength;
Nor longer fear thee or thy brutal force!
A heavenly inſpiration doth aſſure
No ill ſhall 'gainſt a ſpotleſs maid prevail!
The Lybian lion at my feet would crouch,
Tho' hunger-driv'n, if what I've read be true;
Nor murkieſt fiends, nor thou, more dreadful yet,
Can ſoil or harm troth-plighted, clear virginity!

The laſt ſpeech from Caliban reminds one of
the witch's ſon and Florimell, in *The Faerie Queene**
of

* *The Faerie Queene.*—This is the true orthography of Shakſpeare's
time. See the earlieſt editions of that delightful Poem, 4to. 1590, and
1596; in the ſecond ſtanza of which we read, not *Virginn,* but *Virgin.*

" Helpe

of Spenfer ; whom we know Shakfpeare admired, and from whom it is evidently copied : Miranda's reply, if it be not Shakfpeare's writing, was probably founded on a fublime paffage in Milton's *Maſk at Ludlow Caſtle.*

And here muſt I conclude thefe. extracts ; being

"———————— *forbid*
" *To tell the ſecrets of* the *priſon-houſe,*"

wherein the forcerefs Hyrca, and the fpirit of Sycorax, affemble the unhappy voyagers, &c. no,

" *this* infernal *blazon muſt not be !*"

. Whether or not the entire play of *The Virgin Queen* will ever be made publick, I do not know ; nor, if it be not Shakfpeare's, will, I fuppofe, any body care!

F. G. WALDRON.

*January* 28, 1796.

---

" Ilelpe then, O holy *virgin* chiefe of nyne." 1590.
" Helpe then, ô holy *Virgin* chiefe of nine." 1596.
In the " *Deed of Truſt to John Hemynge,*" we read *The Virginn Quene* ; it might as well have been, in the true cockney ſtyle, *The Wirginn Quean.*
The premature ufe of the word *Viewe,* in the fenfe affigned to it in " Viewe o my Maſterre Irelands houfe," will, I believe, fhortly be diſcuſſed, with other congenial topicks, by a much abler pen than mine †
when, if I miſtake not, it will be inconteſtibly proved, thát the orthography of even the name SHAKSPEARE, in the pretended autographs of the Poet himfelf, in Mr. Ireland's volume, is *abſolutely* and *undeniably* WRONG!

# ERRATA.

By a casual omission in page 10, an expression in the paragraph relating to the hand-writing and signature of the Earl of South-ampton's letter, erroneously applies to Shakspeare's letter to the Earl. The reader is requested, therefore, to insert the few words printed below in Italicks, that the passage may stand thus ; ——

The scrawl of *the Earl's answer to* this, sublime and blooming letter, &c.

In p. 32, line 1, for, there's *the* question, read, there's *a* question.

Idem, line 20, for *orderd*, read *ordered*.

In p. 40, instead of, *For a royal Protestant*, &c. read, For a royal Papist to marry a Protestant, as in the case of Henrietta Maria of France, and our king Charles the first, required a dispensation, &c.

---

*Just published by F. G. Waldron,*

The Loves of TROILUS and CRESEID, written by CHAU-CER, with A COMMENTARY by Sir *Francis Kinaston,* from the original MS. never before printed. Price *Two Shilling, and Six Pence.*

*Of whom may also be had, by the same Editor,*

THE SAD SHEPHERD; or, *A Tale of Robin Hood :* a fragment, written by Ben Jonson, With a CONTINU-ATION, Notes, and Appendix.

THE LITERARY MUSEUM ; or, *Ancient and Modern Repository ;* comprising scarce and curious *Tracts, Poetry, Dramas, Biography,* and *Criticism.*

THE BIOGRAPHICAL MIRROR ; comprising a series of *Ancient* and *Modern English Portraits.*

THE ANCIENT and MODERN MISCELLANY ; or, *Shakspercan Museum.*

HEIGHO FOR A HUSBAND ! a Comedy in Four Acts.

THE PRODIGAL : a serious Drama, in Two Acts.

Both acted, with great applause, at The Theatre-Royal, in the Hay-market.

---

Likewise Mr. IRELAND's Volume of MISCELLANEOUS PAPERS, &c.